P9-CNC-892

# Liam Goes Poo in the Toilet

A Story about Trouble with Toilet Training

Jane Whelen Banks

Jessica Kingsley Publishers
London and Philadelphia

First published in 2009
by Jessica Kingsley Publishers
116 Pentonville Road
London N1 9JB, UK
and
400 Market Street, Suite 400
Philadelphia, PA 19106, USA

*www.jkp.com*

**Library of Congress Cataloging in Publication Data**
Banks, Jane Whelen.
    Liam goes poo in the toilet : a story about trouble with toilet training / Jane Whelen Banks.
        p. cm.
    ISBN 978-1-84310-900-6 (pb : alk. paper)
    1.  Toilet training--Juvenile literature.  I. Title.
    HQ770.5.B36 2009
    649'.62--dc22
                                    2008017639

**British Library Cataloguing in Publication Data**
A CIP catalogue record for this book is available from the British Library

ISBN 978 1 84310 900 6

Printed and bound in India by Replika Press Pvt. Ltd.

# Dedication

To Liam: Through whose eyes I have learned to see the world in a different light.

# Acknowledgment

I would like to acknowledge Nancy Ship, who, through the Hanen Course, showed me that for some, pictures could speak clearer than words. I would like to thank her for her support and optimism on cloudy days, and for sharing her time and expertise so generously. Her dedication to children is an inspiration for all.

Successful toilet training is a time of celebration for both parents and child. It marks the end of dirty diapers and a forward step in the development of our child as he begins to create his autonomous self. It is tangible evidence of our success as parents, and memories of this momentous occasion will remain in our hearts.

Fraught with both stress and triumph, the period of toilet training can take from days to months. For a typical child, learning to gain control over the body's internal stimuli can be, at best, challenging. For many children, however, these internal cues can be overwhelming and confusing, leading to both a frustrating and traumatic toileting experience.

**Liam Goes Poo in the Toilet** illustrates the relationship between eating and excreting. It provides visual instructions on how to "relax and push". After much fan-fare, Liam finally masters going "poo" in the toilet, and both he and Mom bask in the glory of a "job" well done.

This is Liam.

Every day, Liam eats lots of good food.

Each time Liam eats, his tummy gets fuller...

...and fuller...

...and fuller

until Liam's tummy starts to stretch...

...and ache.

That means it is time to sit on the toilet
and try to go poo.

We don't run around and try to hold
our poo in our tummy.

We don't go poo in our pants.

Instead, we sit quietly on the toilet...

relax, and push.

Et voilà!

Good job, Liam!